THE FEROCIOUS BEAST

WITH THE POLKA-DOT HIDE

BETTY PARASKEVAS

ILLUSTRATED BY

Michael Paraskevas

Harcourt Brace & Company

SAN DIEGO   NEW YORK   LONDON

Library of Congress Cataloging-in-Publication Data
Paraskevas, Betty.
The ferocious beast/Betty Paraskevas; illustrated by Michael Paraskevas
—1st ed.   p.   cm.
Summary: After outsmarting the beast that was planning to eat him,
a piglet stays on to cook for the beast.
ISBN 0-15-200838-1
[1. Pigs—Fiction. 2. Diet—Fiction. 3. Stories in rhyme.]
I. Paraskevas, Michael, 1961–   ill. II. Title.
PZ8.3.P162Fe   1996
[E]—dc20   95-1847

First edition
A B C D E

PRINTED IN SINGAPORE

The illustrations in this book were done in acrylics on canvas.
The display type was hand-lettered by the illustrator.
The text type was set in Artcraft.
Color separations by Bright Arts, Ltd., Singapore
Printed and bound by Tien Wah Press, Singapore
This book was printed with soya-based inks on Leykam recycled paper,
which contains more than 20 percent postconsumer waste and has a
total recycled content of at least 50 percent.
Production supervision by Warren Wallerstein and Ginger Boyer
Designed by Michael Farmer

To Kate Greer: Well done, dear Kate

To Moucci: A vital member of the team

—B. P. and M. P.

THE FEROCIOUS BEAST with the polka-dot hide
Caught a piglet for lunch. As he tried to decide
Whether to have him on whole wheat or rye,
The poor piglet heaved a sorrowful sigh.

"You're overweight. I fear the worst.
The seams on your hide are about to burst."

"Oh, what should I do?" the ferocious beast cried.
"I'm nothing at all without my polka-dot hide."

"Let me fix your meals, and you will soon be
Fit as a fiddle, I guarantee."
The beast agreed, and the piglet set about
Mixing up parsnips and sauerkraut.

"That's awful!" roared the beast. "I want tiger soup
And takeout from the fast-food chicken coop."

"If you want to save your hide," said the piglet to the beast,
"You must try to eat the foods that you like the least."
"I'll try," replied the beast, and the very next day,
He ate a pail of prunes and a bale of hay.

The poor beast groaned all through the night,
And the next day he had no appetite.

"Try my pine needle salad," urged the piglet. "I think
Your huge polka dots are beginning to shrink."
"No, I'm too weak to eat. I just want to sleep."
And the ferocious beast collapsed in a heap.

That was the piglet's chance to run—
He'd tricked the beast, the deed was done.
But something was wrong. He felt no pride,
Tricking a beast with a polka-dot hide.

So instead of running, he placed a cool cloth
On the beast's aching head, and he made fresh broth. . . .

With celery and carrots he coaxed him to eat,
And the beast was soon back on his feet.

"I'm so hungry," he said, "I could eat a horse."
Then he laughed and added, "I'm kidding, of course."
And as hard as that clever piglet tried,
Nothing satisfied the beast with the polka-dot hide.

Till one day they discovered a pumpkin patch.
The piglet made soup and mixed up a batch
Of pumpkin gruel and pumpkin bread.
"Maybe this will fill you up," the piglet said.

"Oh, it's really delicious!" the ferocious beast cried.
"It just might be the food that will save my hide.
From now on I'll eat nothing but pumpkin for dinner."
And he kept his word, and was healthy and thinner.

The piglet stayed on and in the end,
He was more than a cook—he was a loyal friend
To the polka-dot beast. And now you know
Where the thousands of leftover pumpkins go.